This is a shockingly different look at life through the eyes of someone who saw most of the things happen or had friends that these things happened to.

So let's take a journey into a world of heaven and hell.

You can choose which one you lived or are trying to live.

Thanks to my Mother and Father
Winifred Martin, Andrew Martin he was
the best keyboard man in Detroit both
my parents gone too soon.

My Sister Nichole A. Martin/Parker
and my Junior High School teacher
Judy Kline for believing in me at
thirteen years old and letting me
know English was easy for me.

A shout out to my entire Family
and special thanks to Eddie Thompkins III for all his
help.

# THE BLOCKS

by Andrea. R. Martin

# Table of Contents

# CHAPTER 1

The brick houses on Cheryl's street were decent, the people friendly, their homes represented them, nice neat lawns, fenced in yards with healthy dogs patrolling them. Everyone seemed to keep their shutters and porch railings painted.

The perfect middle-class place to grow up. Teenagers gathered on each others' porches to talk about what each other had done the past weekend. The guys' talked about how many beers they had drank and about the girls they had felt on or planned to, some even discussed in realistic detail about how they had screwed this one and that one!

The girls talked of the guys they liked and how to get his attention with certain hairstyles and different color tight dresses or spandex shorts that they planned to buy, they too discussed sex and how it had been with certain guys and how they wished it could be with others! All the while mothers' cooked delicious dinners, smaller children rode bikes back and forth from corner to corner racing each other, while others played tag or jump rope or different other games to amuse themselves. The men that owned these homes, generally on the same day shift time slot, were returning from a hard days work, looking tired, but glad to be off work, praying upon their arrival their wives (honey-do list) wasn't too long!

A honey-do list is when the wives say honey, would you please do this and honey would you please do that. If none of that was going on, the husbands could sit down for a while or watch the news and relax and unwind until dinner. Usually the men got their way because they were the bread-winners and if they were really tired from work, their wives didn't want to hear them complain!

Cheryl was just coming out of the house on her way to work. She was a secretary at an auto mechanics shop. The guy Ray that owned the shop had hired Cheryl because she seemed to be interested in the business and he loved to teach truly interested people, besides, Cheryl being honey brown complexion, large breast, pretty face and long legs, sandy hair and a beautiful smile, that hadn't hurt either. Cheryl seemed to be a people person and when upset customers came in, mostly men with their complaints, she seemed to soothe them until the matter could be taken care of. Ray respected Cheryl because she was trying to work her way through college. She had just graduated high school and went straight into business college. With four years hard work and a five day schedule of courses, she would have a bachelors' degree and the door to the business world would be open wide! Ray respected Cheryl and her ambitions. Cheryl also helped Ray, when Ray's women 'on the side' called. Cheryl always gave him his messages and never told his wife! Ray had enough women and a wife, so Cheryl was just his secretary!

# CHAPTER 2

The guys that worked in the shop for Ray were Harold, Lenny and Tony, all had set their sights on Cheryl, but she paid them no attention, she just kidded and joked with them. The work situation was easy.

Cheryl had her own office full of records of past clients and future references, all of it she handled with finesse and care. Cheryl was the kind of person you could tell anything and do anything with and nothing was said or gossiped about.

She was a loner, a soft spoken quiet type, seldom, if ever in a qualm with anyone, let's say cute, shy and captivating! All her cards were in order. That described Cheryl. She didn't have a lot of friends, mostly associates and as far as lovers, only two that really stuck out!

In her eighteen years, her first true love was Thomas alias Tico, no one could get to Cheryl like Tico could. He knew how to push most of Cheryl's buttons.

No other guy could do that and Cheryl, even though Tico and she were no longer together, Tico vowed he'd get her back. Tico was trying to make his way in the world. Cheryl knew Tico loved her, he always told her he would return to her with enough stability and moncy to satisfy any need she could possibly have and of course, enough love to drown out any misgivings she might have because their break up should have never happened! Tico wanted to marry Cheryl and swore to her he would do whatever it took to win her back! Cheryl was no fool, she just nodded her head when Tico started this kind of talk, yet and still, Tico kept on swearing as soon as he earned this money, they would be together! Cheryl was not money hungry or a gold digger. Cheryl took everything in life at a patient pace, she seemed older than her years, in a wise, 'I DON'T MAKE TOO MANY MISTAKES KINDA WAY, AND IF I DO I'LL LEARN.'

Cheryl's recently chosen man, Clifton was a hard worker and a ladies man, with his good looks, wavy hair and muscled athletic build; he drove women wild. Clifton claimed he chose Cheryl because they seemed to be working in the same direction and they made a beautiful couple, plus Cheryl fed Clifton's ego. Clifton loved Cheryl's schedule, because she never had a lot of idle time and he always just about knew where she was, and that left no time for her to deal with that Tico guy or anyone else! Man that guy acted sometimes like Cheryl was still his. Well Clifton reasoned, if Tico really irked him he would tell Cheryl not to have anything else to do with him, not even friendly conversation. If that didn't work, Clifton thought, I'll just have to let Tico know who's woman Cheryl actually was' and hopefully the nigger wouldn't want to get that live, but if that was the call, Clifton was really ready because he was tired of Tico's shit anyway. Clifton really wanted Tico's memories erased from Cheryl's mind.

Clifton thought about the whole situation and he started working his jaw muscles and lifting more packing crates to be shipped out of the cannery he worked in.

Clifton picked the stock job because it would keep his arms and waist in shape.

Clifton was proud of his body and he worked on it continuously and all the work showed, all over his body! The women 'oohed' and 'aahed' when he walked down the street in his weight lifters t-shirts and shorts. Clifton loved the attention, so if the women were totally on his jock, some he fucked and some he just teased.

Clifton knew Cheryl would never find out because she was always either at work, in school or studying with a schedule like that. How could she ever catch him doing anything? And, if she did, it would only be because he had slipped up or got careless. Clifton reasoned, if Cheryl caught me, she'd dump me. But with my body and looks, sh-it I can have whoever, I want! Maybe a little pleading might help her to take me back? I'd hate to let a great piece of ass go.  But hell if not, Clifton surmised, 'I CAN ALWAYS FIND SOMEONE ELSE!' Clifton did care about Cheryl, enough to totally keep his extra women a secret, besides they were only warm wet holes any way you look at it!  Clifton thought it struck him funny as he quietly laughed to himself, checking the clock, he only had three more hours of work, then freedom.

# CHAPTER 3

Cheryl's father MR ERNEST D FLEMMING; THE MAN OF ALL MEN, in her eyes, worked as a truck driver carrying everything from appliances to autos from state to state. Mr Flemming loved his job, he'd been driving a truck since he was fifteen years old. First learning on his Dad's truck down south in the fields and back roads. Ernest loved trucking, it allowed his mind to wander, while he was steadily on his way to a different place. He was always playing tourist, sight seeing, meeting new people. Mr Flemming felt he wanted to set foot in as many cities as the world held. He also collected bumper stickers from every city or town he stopped in, not ever sticking them on his truck, the stickers had their own coffee cans with the plastic tops to keep them from getting bent or destroyed in any way.

When Ernest opened his cans of stickers he'd try to remember something special about each place and sometimes even the date he was there. Mrs Flemming, Cheryl's mother just shook her head from side to side when she'd see Ernest with his cans of stickers, she knew he was going on one of his day dream trips. She liked his trips, they didn't cost anything, there was no danger in it and he was still at home while he travelled. You couldn't beat it in her eyes.

Ms. Doris Riley, before marrying Ernest eighteen years ago, had gotten pregnant and told Ernest she would not have a bastard child for him or for anyone else (it was sort of a forced wedding), she said if he didn't marry her she had another fellow who would, so he'd better make up his mind! It didn't take but a week for Ernest to make up his mind after he saw Doris was serious and getting kind of friendly with the oldest Thomson boy, one of the only teenage guys around with his own late model car. Doris never intended on doing anything with the Thomson boy, but Ernest didn't know that. Doris knew Ernest would be furious when he saw the two of them together, and Doris would get exactly what she wanted! Ernest had to wait three weeks before he could buy a ring for Doris because he didn't get paid until then, that was the longest three weeks of Ernest's life. Ernest said he'd be damned before he'd let that Thomson boy and his shiny ride disappear with Doris and his child. Ernest promised Doris he'd give her the world, onto which he knew in his heart he could provide for her and his child. The perfect life. He'd get a great job one day. He'd never be like his friends or anyone else from his neighborhood. Instead of a drunk or a quitter, he'd be a hard worker and a productive husband, and he'd win his wife and child FOREVER! They would be his, no matter the cost. Ernest got his wish and spent the past eighteen years perfecting the craft of being a good husband and father.

Cheryl's classes were starting to get on her nerves. For weeks she pretended the work schedule, the school schedule, the study schedule and family schedule was just fine. She was not pleased with herself or what she had accomplished, it wasn't enough, it seemed to her with all she had done, she hadn't gotten far enough ahead. She didn't make enough money. Even though her parents cherished her, she wanted to be her own person, make her own curfew, be her own judge. She just wanted to be on her own. But that was out of the question, she couldn't afford it right now. The mere thought of Cheryl moving would almost kill her mother. Her father would be totally shocked, considering that she was their only child. They gave Cheryl everything she wanted, Ernest struggled and strived to make sure his only child had everything. He had worked an extra job as a security guard, part time on the midnight shift, just to make sure all of the bills were covered. Cheryl's mother Doris worked when her marriage first began as a housekeeper, scrubbing floors, baby sitting children when she had her mother babysit her child. The couple managed to maneuver themselves into a comfortable status and their one and only is contemplating leaving for heights unknown, to attempt to make her own status, unknown to Cheryl's parents the thought even existed, how could Cheryl be unhappy? Cheryl continued to contemplate the great move, the freedom and the unknown. She would often dream of herself caring for Clifton's baby, the home they'd have. Sometimes Tico's face would replace Clifton's but Cheryl's brain would not accept the thought!

# CHAPTER 4

Tico, his real name Thomas Anton Davis, only close friends really knew his real name, he preferred it that way. Tico wore his name well, he was a pretty boy standing 5'10, medium build with carmel complexion, short curly black hair and a sweet disposition, if he liked you. Tico liked conning people, being slick, psyching women out of their money, hanging out around established people, trying to pick up hints on how to get a lot of cheddar (money) legal. He worked odd jobs lately to keep something in his pockets. Tico thought of all kinds of ways to get money, but none of them were legal and jail didn't really appeal to him. Being more up on life than the people he ganked (used) made Tico feel proud he was smooth enough to pull it off. But Tico was tired of lying to his mother about jobs. Tico's mother Sagrin knew her son was lying about the jobs, but she always held hope for her son Thomas. Sagrin prayed Thomas one day would be a professional somewhere and not end up in a graveyard.

Sagrin Tei, before marriage to Samuel Davis, a marriage that had cost Sagrin, her family, shame and ridicule; all because she married a black man! To Sagrin love had no color. With all the problems her country was facing, it seemed a wise decision, plus Samuel had promised to take her to a new city called Detroit.

Sagrin sometimes had to show the GI's a good time to make money for her brothers and sisters. Sagrin's father had stepped on a land mine a few years earlier, crippling him to the point where he was bedridden. So all the children of the Tei family worked to support the household. Sagrin didn't care for that job but survival was the name of the game so she gritted her teeth every time a GI touched her. With Samuel it had been different, sure he was still a drunken GI looking for a good time but he was not as rough nor degrading as the other GI's she had run across, and Sagrin thought Samuel had the prettiest dark brown eyes she had ever seen on a man. Sagrin had some mixed emotions about leaving her homeland Korea for this place called Detroit.

On his regular drunken weekend of fun with Sagrin, Samuel made Thomas. When Sagrin told Samuel that they were to have a child Samuel froze and looked very hard at Sagrin and uttered not one word. The air was so still, Sagrin swore she could hear the flies buzzing by outside and she was prepared to be beaten for her mistake. Samuel stood very still, then a loud thud crashed on to the table. He had banged his fist on the table in sheer joy! Sagrin had leaped towards the doorway only to be grabbed around the waist and swung up in the air by Samuel, new daddy to be. Sagrin knew right then that she'd follow Samuel anywhere because she knew he loved her. The rest of the night was spent with Samuel telling Sagrin of all riches of living in the Motor City (Detroit). Sagrin believed Samuel and eventually he did bring her and the baby to Detroit after his release from the army.

Almost all of Samuel's bunk buddies told him he was being a dammed fool. Samuel listened with a deaf ear, his heart was set on Sagrin and his child. Samuel and Sagrin with Thomas arrived in Detroit from Korea. Their marriage and living together status lasted two years before Samuel left Sagrin, not for the lack of love, just no money and Samuel's pride could take no more. Sagrin pleaded with Samuel to stay with her and Thomas, but Samuel's spirit was broken and he figured Sagrin could fair better without him. During all the excitement, Sagrin forgot to tell Samuel she was pregnant again. After Samuel left, Sagrin cried hard and she still held their marriage certificate and Thomas, she had no fear of deportation, her only worry was how to take care of her son and the baby on the way.

# CHAPTER 5

Tico hung out as usual with the older guys. These black-men owned their businesses. After closing their various shops some nights, especially on the weekend, it was cocktail hour.  One of the business men kept his shop open and the other shop owners met there to drink, trade secrets, money and lies. Sometimes the neighborhood teenagers came around and sat, it was good fun for everyone because you were only there because you wanted to be. The feeling between everyone was at ease, with the drinks flowing, time to relax, eat, joke or just bullshit. Sometimes Tico did various favors for the shop owners and they didn't hesitate giving him a drink, a joint or pay him a few dollars. The businessmen liked Thomas (Tico) Davis because he was trying to be on the level.

An old class chum named Duck walks up the street, "Hey Tico, what's up?" Tico says nothing, "Old dude, tell me something good." Duck gets this smile, as if he knows it all and nothing at all at the same time, just a plain mischievous grin.

Duck says, "There's these guys a few blocks over man,

booming in the business."

Tico says, "Booming like how? turning a few wrenches, I can do that!."

Duck says, "Naw man they sellin' the ultimate rock!!"

Tico says, "Hey, you know I don't fuck around!!"

Duck says, "Before you talk, I know you got a stash with some cash in it, lets enterprise, fuck these old dudes, they've already made theirs, come on man, so together we can make that kind of money, only we won't be 50 years old when we spend it OK!" Tico ponders for a moment thinking of fine cars, clothes and Cheryl who he knows he can get back with the right tinsel. Tico smiles secret thoughts and would follow Duck to wherever to fulfil his own private fantasies; just follow the Duck to salvation. Tico had waited for this moment, to be introduced right; Tico and Duck walked a few street corners up Fenkell and turned on to Monica about midway the block. They entered the lair of 'The Drake', everyone called him The Drake, I guess it sounded more important or something, who knows? The Drake had seen Tico hanging on the corners in the hood and with different businessmen in the area. He knew what Tico was looking for, just like everyone else, a way out of the ghetto. Some people pick the lottery, some boost clothes, some do B+E's (breaking and entering), some just fuck up and they live and die the measure.

BUT they all want the same thing, out of the ghetto!!! The Drake saw Tico coming up the walkway and knew he had it in him as a runner, a seller, a pick-up man, anything. The Drake had seen it all and this one had promise to be anything he wanted to be! The Drake planned to use this to his advantage. The Drake knew in his own mind that Tico was going to work for him. Tico had a job with The Drake before he even uttered a word!

Tico and Duck entered The Drake's" domain and sat at the dining room table awaiting his entrance. The Drake always had the finest women in the neighborhood before anyone else because of his money and flashy cars and clothes, not to mention his reputation$$$. The young girls and grown women vied for his attention and his affection. The Drake loved all the fuss over him and with so many girls and women around, he didn't have to have a no.1 woman. The Drake fucked whoever he decided he wanted to. Every girl wanted to be 'The Drake's' no. 1……

Coming from upstairs, Drake entered the room where Tico and Duck sat, taking his seat at the head of the table with is back facing the wall. Drake offered Tico and Duck a drink to be brought to them by any of the idle girls standing around. Both accepted beers and eyed the teenage girl Drake sent to retrieve the drinks. While waiting on the drinks, Drake questioned both guys about their backgrounds, even though he already knew you couldn't rub Tico and Duck together and get fifty dollars. More reason why they'd work plenty hard to keep from wearing fast food uniforms, even though those jobs would definitely hold a better future for them.

Because you could file taxes and be a living part of America's hard working class, that way would be too much like right. Besides hamburger slinging hoes didn't drive BMW's; they just look at them through the drive-in window – who wanted to be one of them when you could be the motherfucker driving past them! Drake saw the gleam of greed in both men's eyes. Drake decided to make both of them squirm, while he dangled a carrot before them. Drake suggested he might have a job for Tico. At the mention of that, Duck began to squawk about how he brought Tico there and everything, and how he could be a real asset to the organization.

Drake casually listened to Duck's rendition of 'I WANT TO WORK TOO', then after a while Drake agreed to let

Duck work also, but Duck didn't know Drake would never let Duck and Tico work together because friends working side by side, never ride long on his train; they always try to steal money or dope or both! Drake usually just had the people killed or maimed them depending on how much product was lost. Drake knew a lot of guys like Tico and Duck; they all thought they were so slick. If you put 'em in a grease factory they wouldn't slip, 'bullshit'. Drake knew better, he'd handle the whole situation and it would go as smooth as usual. Drake didn't fear jail because he knew he wasn't going before he shut the lips that were trying to put him there. Drake explained he would give Tico and Duck the addresses to their on-the-job training spots the next day. Both guys left Drake's house slapping hands in high spirits, heads big as watermelons swollen from the thought of all that money they were going to make $$$.

# CHAPTER 6

Cheryl seemed to be getting depressed by all the daily events in her life. First thing of the day, which for any women is a task of making herself presentable, then help mom with breakfast, then if time permits make sure all homework was done correctly. Then off to college to deal with those people. After her three, two hour classes, it's time to report to Ray's auto shop to work some more.

See, in the neighborhood you learned that everyone, whether they did the same thing as you or not, even if they were goody two shoes, Drake knew eventually they would come to him as much as they hated him. If you lived in the neighborhood and were about something or had any kind of guts or gumption, you ended up there, or with one of the lesser dealers working the hood. Because everyone wanted to make it big, the only question was just how bad did they want to do it? Everyone seemed as if they wanted it bad, but only a few applicants fit the bill and Tico and in Drake's eyes completely fit the bill. Tico was now part of Drake's clan, he hated what he was about to do, but money was scarce. So everyone had to what they had to do!!

Tico wanted his mother and brothers and sisters to be proud of him. He especially wanted to be proud of himself? Tico was the man of the house. Ever since his father left he had been trying to help his mother out, but it just wasn't enough. Now Tico had a real chance!!

# CHAPTER 7

Cheryl was sleeping a little, she rarely had time for Clifton or herself; this bothered Cheryl. She knew if you planned on keeping any man you had to be there on the spot. She noticed certain times when she and Clifton were out that certain women stared and elbowed each other when they walked past or talked loud to get his attention. Cheryl could see why the women would be attracted to his handsome face and perfectly toned body, that was the same thing that had caught her attention. It was the lust and hunger in the womens' eyes that troubled her, she tried not to let it bother her, but it always did. Though she said nothing about it to Cliff, he always acted like he didn't see them. Cheryl knew he couldn't help but notice them. Cheryl was proud that Clifton was her man and stuck by her, with all that body and fine too.

Cheryl remembered the day she and Cliff met. Renee a friend of Cheryl's invited her to a pool party. Renee's parents had just had a pool installed and Renee wanted to break it in, in style! So she got her parents OK and threw a gig (party).

Renee invited everyone, and with free food and beer, you know the whole neighborhood and some came!!! Renee's only rules were no fighting and everyone had to wear some kind of swim attire. It was one of those ninety degree Detroit nights, perfect! The music flowed, beer and other drinks were sucked down by the crowd. Women in bikinis, guys either in trunks or cut-offs. Cheryl was too shy to wear a bikini so she wore a black one piece, but that suit didn't hide not one curve of Cheryl's body. Cliff spied her talking with the girls that lived on her block. He watched her for a half hour to see who she was with and he questioned some of the fellas at the party about her. All he got was Tico's girl; shit thought Cliff, where is this Tico? After a while Cliff said to himself, 'fuck Tico' and went to ask Cheryl to dance. When he introduced himself all Cheryl could see was a beautiful smile, large biceps and skin tight spandex trunks and whatever he had in them had to be suffering! Cheryl caught her breath short just looking at this magnificent creature. Cliff had his hand stretched out to her as he talked so she could take it and be guided to the patio to dance. Cheryl was hesitant but her girls whispered she'd be crazy not to go, besides it was only a dance. Cheryl went with Cliff, they danced to a fast record then one of those slow grind songs came on filling the humid night air.

Cliff looked a little too dam eager for Cheryl, SHE COULDN'T JUST let him grind his unknown self against her, she backed out of that dance. If Cliff pursued her, Cheryl knew then she would give in to his whims, but not without a fight He did pursue her all night and before it ended Cheryl did social with Cliff BUT not the grind, the slow I WANT TO GET TO KNOW YOU kind of dance. And that started the romance!

Cheryl sighed contemplating the thought of Cliff while sitting at a study table. She was in between classes, supposedly studying. She vowed she would call Cliff after she got settled in at Ray's shop to see what he was doing tonight when she got off work. She'd just love to hold him close and listen to his plans for their future, while they caressed and undressed to have a fucking good time. Cheryl knew that would keep Cliff coming back always!

# CHAPTER 8

Sagrin was coming out of the grocery store, desperately looking for a jitney to take her home with her groceries, when a beat-up truck pulls right up in front of her.

She stares at the driver angrily till he emerges from the truck. Its Sargent with this big shit eating grin on his face. Sagrin hugs him as he approaches. Sergant is explaining to her he just bought this piece of truck for hauling to make money, as he loaded the groceries onto the back. Sergant told Sagrin the children had told him where she was and he wanted to surprise her. Sergant really didn't let her say anything, he just explained how his situation was going to change, as he climbed into the truck and settled in still talking. Sagrin put her index finger to his lips to shut him up, then she tenderly kissed him. At that moment Sargent wanted Sagrin under him, god knows he was in need as he started the truck, he said nothing else.

Sargent's hand shook slightly as he stopped at a red light. He thought how could he be so lucky to have a woman that loved him, regardless!!! It seemed as if an eternity had passed before he could get on his feet again.

Yet Sagrin waited, he couldn't understand it, but then again he could, he knew she truly loved him through his triumphs and defeats. Sagrin knew when they arrived at the house Sergant would give the kids some money to go to the store with. The kids would beg her to let them go, she would say OK and the house would be cleared and quiet. Sagrin put the refrigerated groceries up when the house cleared. The rest of the groceries would have to wait because it would be time for Sergant's 'ole urgent battle cry', the war Sagrin always won!

# CHAPTER 9

Anthony hung out at the pool hall all the time, so he knew it was just about a sure win for himself, he just needed a pigeon. Clifton decided he'd shoot some pool to relax. As he walks into the room, Anthony spots him and starts toward his unsuspecting pigeon. Cliff spoke to Eddie the manager and to a few of the guys already shooting. Anthony called to Cliff to see if he wanted to shoot a game. Cliff nodded yeah. Anthony put all the balls back on the table. The game was on. Clifton loved chancing his luck, so he bet Anthony ten dollars on the game. The thought of the money made Anthony smile to himself. The name of the game was last pocket. Anthony broke the racked balls making a striped ball, his next shot he made another ball, but he scratched on the cue. Clifton's first shot sunk one of his balls and he missed on his next shot. During the game, Anthony's shots were mostly precise. Clifton's shots were luck and awkward. At the end of the game Anthony had the eight ball and Clifton still had two balls on the table. Anthony grinned and laughed at Clifton's attempt to sink the two balls or even one in any pocket, to no avail. Anthony strutted around the table telling Clifton that the game had been nice and he'd better get that money ready, also he knew that Clifton could never whip him on any table. Anthony posed and talked big shit during the preparation of that last shot. As Anthony aimed, and with medium speed on the cue released the shot, the cue hit the eight ball and, as Anthony expected, the eight went straight into the side pocket, the cue bounced off one of Clifton's balls and slowly fell into the pocket at the other end of the table. Upon seeing this Clifton cracked up laughing. Anthony stood there stunned, completely in shock. Then his anger set in, with that came the excuses. Clifton threw up both his hands in holy praise of the great pool shark, some of the guys on the sidelines were laughing, seeing Anthony beat himself on a table! Anthony shoved his hand into his pocket and pulled out the crumpled bills, he located his one and only ten dollar bill and tossed it on the table.

Clifton knew Anthony didn't work anywhere and ponded the thought of letting slide with the money.

Anthony said, "I know I can beat you, you only won because you're a lucky motherfucker."

That made Clifton snatch the money off of the table and tell Anthony to shut up and quit being a sore ass looser!

and if Anthony had twenty dollars left they could play for double or nothing. Clifton knew Anthony didn't have twenty dollars left, and what he did have, he wasn't going to risk it on a pool game. Anthony said he didn't have time to play another game, he was just going out to hustle up some more money so he could get blowed later on that night. Clifton joked with Anthony that he was lucky he had to go to pick up Cheryl from work. Both Clifton and Anthony slapped hands and walked to the door together. Anthony made up his mind he needed more money and he was headed straight to one of the Blackman's houses to see if he could get a job with him. Anthony was tired of being broke, busted and discussed he need steady money so he could get his shit together and right now Blackman seemed to be his ticket.

# CHAPTER 10

Tico returned from home after his meeting with The Drake. Tico acted as if he were high on something, all that played through his mind were thoughts of being able to help his mom and his brothers and sisters, and still have money for a badass ride with large speakers in the trunk. Don't forget he needed some fresh clothes to sport around in his ride, then Cheryl would really be impressed and ditch the other dude she was messing with, whatever his name was. That thought put a frown on Tico's face, only for a moment, because in his mind he had the master plan of how you win this life game.

Sagrin came out of her bedroom when she heard Tico come in. She knew if Tico had known Sergant was in the house the roof would hit the heavens. Tico didn't care at all for his father, the man had left his mom when he was small, so he figured why should he like him? Sergant had never really been there for Tico. All Tico really had know all his life was Sagrin his mother. Tico loved her deeply and figured his mother only still slept with Sergant because that was all she was use to or had known. Secretly Tico really didn't mind his separated parents fucking because at least all his brothers and sisters had the same father. Tico really hated his father for not suffering and taking the hard knocks like some fathers did with their families. Tico was older now and he didn't need a father, the younger kids in his family respected his opinions, taunts and playful affections, besides Tico was the oldest of all of Sagrin's children and the greatest in his siblings eyes.

Sagrin caught up with Tico in the kitchen, she just told Tico his father was in the house, his facial expression changed for a moment then he looked at his mom with contempt, kissed her hand and forehead and told her he had found a job that might take them out of the ghetto and possibly, once she fixed herself up she could find a guy who would really love her and would stay with her forever. Then Tico turned back to the counter and continued making his salami sandwich. Sagrin was shocked, but said nothing because whatever kept Tico calm was good enough for her, even a visit from Sergant couldn't fuck up Tico's happy feelings today.

# CHAPTER 11

The Drake phoned Blackman. Blackman was just as heavy in the game as the Drake. They both made a pact to be alliances for each other so relatively they were unstoppable. Between the two separate groups there were at least three hundred and fifty people in each, not including the spies in the streets that would bust on their own mommas for a few dollars. Usually when they had a beef with another rival drug ring, it was a damn massacre. Both Blackman and Drake's guys would become brothers and fight side by side, the agreement had its perfect meaning and it was, that you don't fuck around Fenkell Way unless you damn near had the National Guard behind you in full dress. Blackman phoned Drake back. Drake suggested it was time for them to throw a block party and possibly get some more new recruits, and Drake mentioned he had just hired Duck and Tico.

Blackman said, "Damn man, I was waiting on Tico to fall in step. I knew he was because aint shit else out there to do and make a trunk full of money quick but that damn Duck is going to be a problem and you know it!"

Drake said, "I know the punks in for a bullet, might as well let him think for one time in his life he's going to be on top of the world, besides, anyway Duck brought Tico with him, so he is almost worth something."

Blackman said, "That's good, but which block are we thinking of taking over? What about Tuller? That block is too short, shit why not Chalfonte?" The Drake said.

Blackman said, "Damn it man, that street is almost as busy as Fenkell with traffic."

The Drake said, "We'll have some of the boys lift some barricades and construction shit for us to block the street."

Blackman said, "Yea, that ought a work, lets fire this thing next Saturday and then that will give us some time to get all the bullshit we need to pull this off."

Blackman said, "I just got one question, what you giving the fuck block a party for?"

The Drake replied, "A good businessman always puts on a good show and looks like he's giving something back to the community, when in actuality he's taking even a bigger piece of pie, because people begin to trust and like Him!"

Blackman replied, "You know what, your damn right, we'll go out looking like tide on new whites and maybe people won't call the boys in blue. So much trying to shut down the spots?"

"I hope it works" Drake replied.

"It will" Blackman retorted, "Well, I got to go Drake I need some new rims for my ride. I bent one last night, so catch you later, peace!"

Drake hung up the phone very pleased with himself and his plan.

# CHAPTER 12

Cheryl was just doing the last bills for Ray. Ray himself lounging on the customers' service sofa, his legs stretched out, hands folded behind his head as the president of the successful company usually does at the end of a busy day.

Ray says, "Well Cheryl, we end another week, you know I was thinking I deserve something special for all my efforts in this business, I think in a couple of days, I'm going to go to the car dealership and order me a brand new Triple Black Lincoln town car. Watcha think?"

Cheryl pondered, then said, "If that's what you want and you can afford it, that's sweet, since we are doing so well, how about a raise?"

Ray smiled with his gold tooth sparkling in the light and said, "If everything

continues to boom around here, I promise you, you'll get a raise."

Yea sure I will as she put money into the cash register settling a bill and lifted an eyebrow at Ray in disbelief.

I'm sure you have plenty of things to do before I get my raise when Tony walked into the lounge area hollering, Smokey Robinson's, Ooo Baby, Baby!" and dancing around Cheryl, Cheryl laughing at him because he had a candy bar half hanging out of his mouth and every time he said something, little bits of peanuts and chocolate would fly out of his mouth.

Cheryl said, "I know you aren't trying to be sexy", even though she still continued to laugh at him.

Tony just said, "You know you have never been sung to so good, your just jealous because yo man don't sound like me, but see I'll give you this one time offer, you can have all of me for free, hows that?"

Cheryl said, "Get serious Tony and you'd better not let Robin, your pregnant woman hear you talking like that. I heard she wears you out when she wants to, ha, ha."

Ray commented he'd heard the same story.

Tony, to protect his manhood said, "Shit, Robin do just what I want her to."

Ray said, "Yeah, as long as she don't catch yo in no shit, yo ass is as smooth as Velveeta.

By now Tony's mad because he knows its true, so he just grumbles to himself and walks back to the work area with the whole shop laughing at him. Tony asked Lenny what the fuck he was laughing at.

Lenny replied, "yo ass."

Tony said he didn't see shit funny and how could Lenny laugh when he didn't even have a woman.

Everyone laughed at Lenny, Lenny told Tony he had plenty of women.

Tony started to get nervous and when he got nervous he started to stutter, it went something like, "Shit len-len-lenny, don, don, don kno know sh-sh-shit." That one sentence really cracked up the shop because everyone knew it had to be true what Tony said, because of the way Tony stumbled over his words!

Ray was the first to stop laughing and tell the guys to get back to work, so they could finish up on that car they were working on tonight, then they would have a clean slate to start with tomorrow. That quieted everyone.

# CHAPTER 13

Cheryl got her pay check, one hundred and sixty dollars. After work Ray offered to drive Cheryl home and again promised her a raise soon. No sooner had he said that then Clifton pulled up. Cheryl's face was already flushed from laughing at Lenny and Tony's antics, her eyes were sparkling as she said goodbye to everyone and climbed into the car with Clifton, his smooth sounds kicking out of the radio, a light film of sweat on his brow. As Cheryl settled in, Clifton pulled Cheryl to him and kissed her passionately on the mouth and his hands began to roam on Cheryl's chest and throat. Cheryl knew mentally Clifton was horny and ready for her. She didn't really feel like sex but for Clifton, Cheryl knew she would give into him, besides Clifton always made Cheryl's insides quiver, he was a great lover. Most of Clifton's ex-lovers would fuck him again if given a chance, but right at this moment, Clifton could already picture Cheryl's lovely body beneath his. This thought made Clifton's jeans real tight in the crotch, because he could feel himself begin to rise for the occasion.

Cheryl broke the silence as they rode to Clifton's home with idle chatter about work, none of it Cliff even really heard, his mind set on fucking. Cheryl kept on talking because she was trying to ease that tense feeling she always got just before giving herself to someone; Cliff doesn't use condoms, and Cheryl didn't make him wear them. She always worried about getting pregnant and what would she do if it happened? Would Clifton marry her? Were they really that compatible? How would she finish college? What would happen to her job? Cheryl was thinking real hard. She asked Cliff to stop at a store and get her a pop. Clifton stopped a the first store he saw and jumped out of the car to get the pop. While Cliff was in the store Cheryl began digging in her purse, she had forgotten to take her birth control for a few days and she figured better late than never!

Clifton returned to the car with an orange pop. Cheryl already had her pill in her hand. Cliff opened the pop and handed it to her and continued driving towards his house. Cheryl swallowed the pill with a few gulps of pop. Cliff didn't even notice, his mind set on getting his rocks off. Cheryl felt slightly better after taking the pill but was still unsure of it working, but she didn't want to fight with Clifton over not letting him make love to her.  So she knew in the next hours Clifton would most definitely be getting

is way. Cheryl just prayed that she wouldn't be fucked up

when it was all over!

# CHAPTER 14

Tico and Duck started working at this crack house on Cloverdale. Since neither of the guys were large, they couldn't be bouncers in the smoke rooms. See the way this house was run, Drake had one large dude named Gatman run the front door. The only way you came to the front door was that you had to be a VIP and a very regular person, almost never short on the money, just a straight up business person. If you'd had anything else in mind, such as getting a free bee, wanting a favor or playing stick-up-kid your ass was hit. Gatman didn't want to hear no sob stories, you couldn't get shit free from him and, as for robbery, that was totally out because Gatman didn't trust not one, not a damn soul, he was always ready to pop you when you knocked on the front door. Every now and then a young girl might be in need of a rock or two and have no money. Gatman never left his post at the front door so if he ran up on a new, broke, begging, young female crack head, he might let her in the house. Gatman would walk straight to the couch with her, the door still visible from there. He'd tell the chick she couldn't have but one rock, but she had to blow his head right there. If anyone came downstairs they would see exactly what was going on. Gatman figured if a bitch would do that, they had to be hooked, because he never went near a bathroom before they would start the job! Gatman always told them before they get started that if she sucked him real good, he'd give her an extra rock for doing it perfect. As result he usually got a perfect head job because the thought in the girl's head was, 'if I do my best, he'll give me more'. Gatman always laughed to himself while the young girls worked on him, because he knew, even if she had a 14kt tongue that did tricks, she was only going to get one rock, and he might cut a 10 in half if the girl was really pretty, just to tease her with the other half, but she couldn't get the other half unless she went through the whole ordeal again. Usually, the girls were wet from giving Gatman a head job. To amuse himself he might make them strip and fondle themselves in front of him and anyone else who cared to look. That usually did the trick for Gatman, he never felt sorry for the heads (addicted people) because everyone has a choice, he didn't use rubbers because you can't catch Aids from a hand job, ladies and girls would not kill him with AIDS. He figured he could deal with any of the other diseases because one trip to Herman Keifer hospital and he'd be OK but most of the time Gatman kept his dick in his pants, that was one thing Gatman truly feared! AIDS.

Drake had a tall, skinny guy named Lerch at the back door. Lerch never opened the door, the customers put their money through a slot in the door only big enough for money to fit. You never even saw Lerch, your money went in the slot and your crack came back out. If you had a complaint, you could try your luck at standing out there bitching about the size or whatever and a few guys might come out the front door and take the crack you were complaining about, kick your ass and send you home. They rarely got complaints. If a VIP didn't like the quantity he was given he was allowed another choice, but he or she could only exchange their drugs, right when they were given to them. There was no such thing as you didn't have enough light to see or whatever, you had better see, be sure and everything else, because once you have left it was yours. Lerch wasn't as nice as Gatman, he was the type that seemed as if he was never happy, his face was long and kind of drawn in. Everyone had always teased Lerch because of his height and gangly stature, he constantly had a frown on his face like he was mad. Sometimes Lerch might share a girl with Gatman. If Gatman had had his fill of the girl and she was still in need of more crack, Gatman would holler to Lerch and see if he wanted to handle her. Lerch seemed to have a hatred for people, not just women. If he was in the mood, he'd yell, "send her back." Gatman would get one of the house boys to walk her to the back of the house. Lerch would peer at her from seemingly hooded eyes, checking her from head to toe. He'd always ask the girls to turn around so he could see their asses, the girls would usually be bragging on themselves about how they could make Lerch feel. The girls usually smoked the rock Gatman had given them and that gave them false courage to almost do anything for another one. Lerch had his fantasy that if he degraded a girl enough, maybe she wouldn't smoke crack any more. He always let the girls he was going to teach a lesson to, have one hit off the pipe before he'd tease them with several bags of crack waving at eye level.

He'd stand behind the girls feeling their breast, nipples hardening at his touch. Usually the girls were wet from giving Gatman his hand job. Lerch would rub himself against the girls if they were clean smelling and he'd kiss them on the neck and almost seem as if he is going to really be a special person in their lives. All the while a house guy named Styles stays near the kitchen. He asks Lerch if he needs him to watch the door. Lerch mumbles OK and gives Styles fifteen ten dollar packets. At the same time Lerch is unzipping his pants, still talking softly, and promising the girl more drugs. After they finish, Styles sits right by the slot while Lerch is in the kitchen with this totally nude girl rocking from side to side. Lerch puts on a condom, the lubricated kind. By now the girl has put her trust in Lerch because he really seems nice. Lerch explains to her that he can't really leave his post either. By now he has his condom on, usually the girls get impatient and this always makes Lerch mad. Styles always knows when the action is coming because Lerch's face turns into a scowl and he usually grabs them by their hair and puts her face down on the table. If she moves too much Styles helps hold the girl until Lerch gets into position to fuck her ass. When the girls find out that's what Lerch wants, some scream, some try to run, but all get fucked in the ass by Lerch. Styles watches the girl writhe on the table looking at him with tears, pity and pain in their eyes. If they were to scream too loud Styles usually finds a rag or something to stuff in their mouths and he returns to the back door because he figures the girls ask for that kind of treatment hanging in a crack house.

Styles always gets excited watching Lerch get off on a freak, its something erotic about it to him. The girl is usually crying and pleading with him to stop, but he never does until he's finished teaching the girl his lesson! When he reaches his orgasm, he groans and shakes. By this time the girl is too tired to fight and goes limp on the table. Lerch withdraws himself from her, leans on the wall behind the table, takes off the condom and wipes himself off on her panties and he tosses her her clothes and a ten dollar rock. He takes his place at the back door again as she slowly dresses Lerch always searches their faces to see if they want some more work. Styles hands her an Antenna to smoke her hard earned rock if she doesn't have anything of her own to use. The young girls usually guard their ten dollars packet more than they do their ass, and in this case, its the truth. After smoking that ten, most are glad to give Styles just a pole polish, seems the girls never notice the more sex they give the smaller their prized pieces of crack got!

Tico and Duck experienced all this on their first day. Drake had the two check out how the operation was run. Tico was to work midnights as a shotgun man with Lerch. Duck was to be a houseboy. If the crack heads that smoked in the house got into it, Duck and the other houseboy Eddie were to evict them to the downstairs where they could be thrown out and probably jumped on by the Bouncers if Duck and Eddie didn't do it first! Both Tico and Duck would work different shifts.

# CHAPTER 15

Cheryl and Clifton lay side by side in Clifton's bed. Pictures of bodybuilders adorned his walls, weights on the floor by the dresser, a powerhouse t-shirt tacked to the wall over his bed. Clifton seemed as if he was falling asleep. Cheryl curled herself up against his body both seemingly reminiscent of their past lovemaking session. Cheryl was tired but not sleepy so she had laid in Clifton's arms. Thoughtfully, Cheryl asked Cliff what were they going to do this weekend. He groggily told her 'haven't you heard, there's supposed to be a Bomb Party on Chalfonte tomorrow night.' He thought they'd go since the booze and food were free. Besides, all his friends were going and he reminded Cheryl, all her girls would probably be there too. With that said, Cliff went to sleep. Cheryl laid there so long, with nothing to do, she fell to sleep thinking how bright her and Clifton's future was looking right then.

# CHAPTER 16

The Drake and Blackman had all the party fixings, enough ribs, beer, wine, pop, chips – the works enough to feed an army and they knew they had better be ready to feed the army that was coming to the Block Party bash. The whole neighborhood chattered about the Block Party and all the food and drinks. Some middle aged parents strictly forbade the children to be part of the dealers Block Party. But that party was going to be the place to be. Everyone would appear, even if just to get some of the free food and beer. Both Blackman's and Drake's workers stole road blocking posts from various construction sites. One site on Six Mile and Woodingham was detouring cars from a large pot hole. When Blackman's people removed the blinking yellow yield sign, an older model Buick raced down Six Mile, straight into the large hole causing the axle to break, which made the unsuspecting driver get busted in the face with his steering wheel. As his blood covered him, his car stopped abruptly not able to move any further. A smaller car containing two talkative sisters behind the wheel politely hit it directly in the trunk, smashing the entire front end of their small vehicle, everyone in shock and bloody, but trying to figure how could all this bad luck betail them? One word, Drake!

The Drake had the people who'd do the cooking, male and female, also some to handout the beer and various rap star's posters. It was all set for tomorrow.

# CHAPTER 17

Duck was working his shift at Drake's Indiana joint not far from the Cloverdale Chalfonte House. Everything was relatively quiet, they had some customers about a half an hour ago, but nothing now. Duck talked and tried to get along with the man of this house named Preach. Preach was an OK dude but trigger happy, he carried all his courage in his waistband in the form of a .357 mag with hollow point bullets. One thing about Preach, usually after he finished being angry and preaching a small sermon, he shot your ass if you had crossed him wrong. Preach wasn't a very big man, twenty-three years old, brown complexion, 5'5 inches tall, a hundred and forty pounds. See the .357 made Preach the same size as any man with his reputation. Most stayed clear of him. Crazy motherfucker. The Drake figured if he put Duck with Preach that would keep him in line, Drake knowing Duck had to collect a few pay checks before he'd feel his oats. Also, with Duck and Tico being split up, maybe Drake had hired two great recruits instead of one? Tico was working out just fine, it was only two days ago Tico started but the reports Drake received from Lerch and his other workers on Cloverdale, Tico did exactly as he was told to the tee and worked his twelve hour shifts as expected, doing whatever. Also, Tico had refused to fuck with any of the crack head women running through the house trying to fuck or suck up on a high, he'd just wave them on when they looked his way with that pleading look in their eyes. Drake liked exactly what he heard concerning Tico, Duck on the other hand had been doing his do, letting anything with a mouth suck on him, sometimes giving the women five dollars, a chip off of a ten dollar rock. One chick he knew he could stiff, and he did, giving her nothing for her work. It didn't really matter to Drake, but he wanted Duck to learn you can't dick everything in the world!

Drake made a phone call to a chick called China. Drake told China to send him a girl that was burning hot and gorgeous. She said she'd be over in ten minutes for him, Drake made her understand the circumstances and that the woman was for Duck, one of his workers. China was distressed, The Drake didn't want her to make one of her rare appearances, but understood the call was business. She made Drake promise to see her soon on a personal tip and that she had the perfect person in mind for this guy Duck. Drake gave China the address to where Duck was and the girl was to be there tonight, and if she was, the girl would get fifty dollars from him on completion of her task. China gave her word the girl would be there and with kisses over the phone line bid Drake good-bye.

Drake had to smile at his plan, because he knew after tonight Duck would slow down all of his fucking off, he might fall in love. Drake had to laugh out loud at how clever he really was, but he reasoned the only reason why he'd planned the event was because he really didn't like Duck anyway. No specific reason, Drake just didn't like the guy and the guys Drake didn't like didn't stay working for him too long If Duck really got out of line, Drake would keep him in check!

# CHAPTER 18

The people that lived on Chalfonte between Cherry lawn and Tulles were very excited to see roadblocks being put up. Sure they're just like any other block, had raggedy spots in the pavement, some thought the street were being repaired until they saw large Barbecuing pits being rolled to various parts of the street. These were makeshift stands being put up with banners saying 'Lets Feed the Children' the street was blocked so well the people who lived in the block couldn't park in front of their homes, they had to park wherever and walk to their homes. You couldn't move any of the blockages because between Drake and Blackman they had people at each and every blockage to ensure that it wouldn't be moved! No one argues with a gun, you might not like the turn of events, but you just accept it, unless you were prepared to die right then or be ready to leave your home for a safer one! No one fussed too much!

Soon the music was cranked up and the smells of roasting hot dogs and hamburgers, along with the rib smell, engulfed the place and surrounding streets. Hungry children, their grubby faces, uncombed hair and too small clothing, stood around watching for anything to get done because at home there as absolutely nothing to eat. At last, if they stood long enough someone hopefully would feed them. See if you're a parent, usually it's a single woman on drugs, you don't have enough money for anything else, your mind only seems to work right when you're high, you only feel good when you are high, nothing matters, not the hungry children, bills, rent, food, in other words you'd spend your life's blood to get high. Sometimes crack heads will donate blood for money. Things are almost the same with alcoholics or any substance impaired person. So the children wait while the d-jay spins the top forty, people begin mingling in the streets to kick off the day's event.

# CHAPTER 19

Blackman called Drake. Blackman had come up with a great idea, and wanted to run it to the Drake. Blackman puts 911 at the end of the phone number he'd dialled from so Drake would immediately call him back.

As expected, The Drake called Blackman back. In almost a minute later, Drake had been driving down Seven Mile when his cell phone began to vibrate against his hip. He checked the number as he stopped for a red light. Drake saw the 911 and began dialling Blackman to the return his call. Blackman explained that they should meet somewhere because taking business over phone lines was dangerous for both parties. Drake agreed and told Blackman he'd meet him in twenty minutes at Slow Joe's, that was their code name for a middle-aged bar on Greenfield near Fenkell. Both men knew the Feds or NARCS often listened in on conversations trying to catch anything they could.! The Drake pulled into Slow Joe's lot. People across Greenfield at the bus stop eyeballed the sleek triple black Mercedes with gold detailing and shiny gold rims. As the Drake closed his sunroof, teenage girls were walking by, no more than fifteen years old, giggling and trying to talk loud so The Drake would pay them some attention. With the loud distraction, Drake stared right at the cluster of girls. All seemed willing to go anywhere with him.  By the look in their eyes, it said 'hungry or I'm game', but Drake never bothered chicken wings (that's what he called young girls) and after they passed, Drake finished locking up his car with the remote on his key chain and entered Slow Joe's. It was dark and cool, seemingly just right because of the hot, thick, steamy air outside. Drake settled in at the bar and ordered a beer. It was too hot outside even to think of drinking liquor. Not long after Drake received his beer, Blackman entered. Blackman spotted Drake at the bar and sat next to him. Both men said their greetings while slapping hands and making small talk. Blackman also ordered a beer. This was delivered and the barmaid left the two men. The Drake asked Blackman if he was making too much money?

Blackman replied, "Hey I make my share, but what nigger couldn't stand a little more?"

The Drake said he was sending everyone of his people, plus some to sell weed and give testers to every person possible at the Block Party and what did Blackman think about that?

Blackman haunched his shoulders and said, "So?"

The Drake said, "I know that's no big deal, but there's a catch. Everyone that buys joints or bags will get a special kick, the weed has been laced with heroin and will be sold at the regular price. No one will know, they just want to get high!"

Blackman said, "Shit man, what you trying to do, go broke?"

The Drake replied, "Naw man, just gathering up some new customers."

Blackman looked at The Drake and said, "Well how?"

The Drake said, "Easy man, with everything being free at the Block Party, you know people, if its free they say give me, even if they don't need the shit. If they take the free joint and return to buy more, you got them. Heroin is a fast worker, if you don't mind, it don't matter!"

Blackman said, "Damn man, you thought that shit through to the very end didn't you. Man as long as the shit ain't to heavy in the weed, they won't know and after a joint or two, they won't care! Ha! Ha! Ha!. Man that's on the money. I guess you gotta spend some to make some!" Blackman said he would send most of his boys down to the Block Party to ensure that everyone that smoked that night, would be as high as hell!. The Drake ordered Blackman another beer. While he did that Blackman text out a five number code that let his workers know what he wanted done. Blackman's attention was back to The Drake. He had the biggest grin on his face and held his hand out for The Drake to shake, to which he did, smiling.

Also then, both men raised their beers in the air clinking them together and said, "Partners Forever". Each man took a long swallow, both of them thinking of the new customers and hoping there were thousands of them.

# CHAPTER 20

Tico had previously told The Drake he needed to make more money, and he had a draw plan on exactly how to make himself not expendable. This is what The Drake was calling this meeting for. The Drake wanted everyone to bite the bait. Tico had given The Drake a draw plan fully mapped out, step by step, on how to take over Detroit and never have to look back. The Block Party was just the first action to start a chain reaction no city has seen before! The Drake told Blackman about the deal and Blackman agreed that it was a hell of a play and he was in!

Two days later, all the leaders of every gang of runners, small time thieves, even the B+E's wanted in. The plan was simple, everyone unite into one and that force would be so powerful, also unstoppable! An off the top of the head count of how strong soldiers that were behind The Drake now was about 25 – 30,000 people. As long as everyone got paid it was all good. And the policemen of Detroit were fucked, they were powerless to that many people working together to get money and keep the police off track and out of the loop of exactly what was really going on in the "D".

Blackman and The Drake's personnel were busy at work, lacing joints and preparing packages for the runners to distribute. The Block Party was underway, the hot dogs were done first and it seemed every child anywhere near the Block Party munched on a hot dog full of smiles, grins and laughter. Some parents scolded their hungry children for accepting food from the different booths, the children shrugged their shoulders and ducked flying hands aimed at their heads for disobedience, still all the while running, wolfing the hot dogs and pop down with knowledge that all the food that wasn't eaten at this party, would never be!

Because if you waited to eat when you got home, you'd starve because there was nothing there, most of the time the cupboards were bare.

The Drake's crack workers were in full swing, stripped of regular clothes, only wearing paper-pants with a drawstring, sort of made like medical wear but not expensive. No men or women had on shirts, The Drake figured the less clothes, the less chance of theft he faced from the workers. They were producing extra crack so there would be no shortage, even with The Drake's extra activities concerning the party.

Everyone was preparing for the Block Party. Even if

you didn't live on the Block, you wanted to make your appearance. Hell, The Drake was giving the party and he didn't live on the street either. Just his crack houses and weed joints. But most, if not all, his customers lived in the vicinity!

# CHAPTER 21

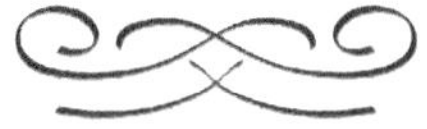

Cheryl had called Clifton and they decided to wear black outfits, not alike but sort of the same color, I guess it proved some kind of togetherness. They decided at dusk to head to the Party. Even Cheryl's co-workers, Lenny, Tony and Harold were going to the Party and bringing their women, because it was a free night and those don't come too often. If you say free, everyone says me!. Clifton arrived at Cheryl's on time, like he said, dressed in a black muscle shirt, with black jeans. Cheryl came out of the house waving good-bye to her parents, smiling wide, dressed in a sexy black crop top and frayed black shorts. As she entered Cliff's shining car he smelled, a new perfume Cheryl had on, and instantly it went straight to his crotch. Clifton said if it wasn't for this Party hell he'd be glad just to spend a night alone with Cheryl with her smelling that good!

Cheryl said I know the advertisement said, 'Drive your Man Wild', but she never knew it would work and she was glad he liked or rather loved it. She also put the question to Cliff, 'what did I smell like before?!'

Cliff laughed and said, "You know you always stunk

real good, but this is just exceptionally good funk!"

Cheryl hit at Clifton as they pulled off down the street. It seemed as if everyone was arriving on Chalfonte at the same time, finding a reasonable place to park was a bitch, but for free everything, people parked and walked to the scene. You could hear the music the DJ was slamming on for three of four blocks. The party looked like big family cook out. They even had game booths. For a quarter or fifty cents you could play and win stuffed animals or small kiddie toys. All the proceeds would be donated to childrens' clubs in the surrounding area.

Sagrin and Tico's two brothers and sisters were milling around from stand to stand. Sagrin didn't like the event but you couldn't help but be curious about the whole thing and there was just no keeping the children away from the party, so she chose to attend the gathering rather than wonder what her children were getting into. Even Sargent had heard about the Party and planned to check it out.

After parking, Clifton and Cheryl were busy saying hello, waving to others, making their way to Chalfonte on foot like everyone else. The atmosphere was so festive, happy, warm and inviting. No one argued, fussed or made a scene, it was just time to party! Cheryl wanted some ribs. Cliff was trying to talk her out of eating that pork, but Cheryl reasoned that if she had been eating pork all her life, this time wasn't going to make a difference! Cliff gave up and just frowned when she bit into the rib sandwich handed to her by one of the helpers. Cliff did secretly think those ribs damn looked good, but now he couldn't relent on his beliefs after putting up such a fight.

# CHAPTER 22

Tico was putting the finishing touches to his new outfit. The Drake had fronted him some money ahead of his pay schedule for his event. Tico was thankful to The Drake for that. The job, just a chance, but Tico knew he couldn't work in that trade for long, besides he had given the Drake a key to riches, but for now it would have to do even if it was against his principles. Shit the two hundred dollar silk pants suit he was looking at hanging on the door, wouldn't be there without it! Besides Cheryl's gonna flip when she sees him. With that thought he slapped on some cologne on his chest and hot spots while grinning at himself in the mirror!

Duck received a call on his cell phone that told him to hold tight where he was at the Indiana Spot. He wondered what he had done now! And if he had to stay, would he be paid for the extra time he had to spend there. Shit he thought, its the end of my shift and now they call saying hold on. He wondered if he'd ever get to party like everyone else was doing right now. About three minutes later Preach called Duck to the door. When he came Preach told Duck it was a bitch at the door for him. Duck looked out the peephole and couldn't believe his eyes, this woman was so fine. All Duck could do was to tell Preach to let her in. Preach asked where Duck knew her from. Duck played it off and said he had been trying to talk to her a few days ago. Preach opened the door and Ms. Fine walked in, she seemed to know Duck, so Preach thought nothing else, but he knew if he'd seen her anywhere, he would have tried to pull up on her too. After she entered both men seemed to stare. Duck, seeing Preach's eyes wonder over her body, pulled her to the side out of ear shot to find out her name and how he could be so lucky. At that moment Duck knew he was the man and this woman would be his tonight. Fuck that damn party! Duck quickly asked her name and she leaned on his shoulder and whispered in her subservient voice, Sharon. The way she said her own name made the hair on his neck stand up amongst other things! Shit how lucky could one man be? Sharon had a shape that women kill for, beautiful eyes seemingly turquoise right now, dark brown hair, straight with just a hint of curl on the ends and a soft toffee complexion with a perfect smile and teeth that could have been capped, they were so straight. She asked Duck for a ten dollar rock and the only reason she had asked for him at the door was because the streets said he was moving up in the world and what woman wouldn't want a man who worked in the game with up and coming big dollars to follow him? As she lit up part of the rock he had given her, after blowing the smoke out, Duck and Sharon moved to the den. Business was slow so Duck had plenty of freedom. As Sharon talked, Duck knew she was no crack head, the woman had style and class and it seemed as if she owned all of it, those words were made just for her! Duck reasoned, even if she did smoke a little, shit everyone had a quirk or two, she was worth the rock he had given her and very last one in his pocket! Sharon told Duck spots where drugs are sold made her nervous to hang out in and asked when would he be getting off?

Duck told her to hold on, he'd check. Duck got up off the couch, found Preach and asked him to call The Drake to see if he could go. His shift was over half an hour ago. Preach called while Duck was standing there. The Drake OK'd Duck to leave. Before Preach hung up Duck also asked Preach to see if it was alright for Duck to have a small advance? To Duck's surprise, The Drake OK'd fifty dollars. Preach had never seen such contempt on a niggers face waiting for that answer, but when the green light was given, sweat bands seemed to pop off that niggers head. Shit if a bitch like that was waiting on him, he would be fucking right now! So Duck was trying to be straight. Preach gave Duck fifty dollars and took all the packages of crack he had, he had 12 in all. When Duck re-entered the room Sharon had just finished smoking and sitting there fine as ever awaiting his return!

Duck told her, "lets ride if you're ready."

Sharon got up, straightened her skirt, patted her hair and asked Duck where was his car parked. Duck paused and told her his buddy had it and if she had a car they would have to use hers because he thought he would be working tonight, so he leant it out.

Sharon had a car parked several houses from the dope spot. Everyone knows you never park in front of a dope house your visiting, too much shit happens at them.

Sharon had an old Cutlass in nice condition. She asked Duck to drive saying she loved to be chauffeured around and she wanted to get something to eat. Duck knowing he only had fifty dollars suggested they go up the street to the party his people were giving and eat them out of house and home. Sharon was cool with it, so they headed three or four blocks up to the party. If they weren't serving watermelon they could damn sho' use Duck's head because it was big enough to feed everyone. Duck couldn't wait for his friends to see him now!

# CHAPTER 23

Tico was a finished product and he looked like a toy still in the box on Christmas morning. As he left the house he surmised his family was on Chalfonte having fun. It was dark now but porch lights and street lights lit the way. Tico was entering from the Livervois end and Duck and Sharon were entering from the Greenlawn end of the party. Everyone was there, old and young, there was so much to eat there was no need to hog one stand seeing as how there were so many. Even The Drake was turning off of Fenkell on to Tuller to make his great appearance with his bevy of beauties and henchman. As his long silver limo pulled up to the Tuller blockade, seeing the children and their mothers rush to his car made him lurch. Seeing everyone clamour around his car, The Drake put on his dark glasses and said to everyone, 'Look at all my people' as he exited the car and began shaking hands and waving at everyone. The thought hit his mind, 'Shit, I must be President, maybe one day I'll run for office?'

That day didn't seem like all the rest, there was a some kinda electricity in the air, it was like you knew something was about to happen but you didn't know what exactly, but you were excited any way. The Drake had never been prouder of himself, he also knew something was in the air, it smelled like money and lots of it. The Block Party boomed, there were smiles on everyones' faces, the music flowed. The Drake was in his realm. That night everyone adored him, the drug addicted mothers loved him for feeding her kids, the drunks for the free beers and the regular people, they just appreciated the party.

Duck pulled up in Sharon's old Cutlass and checked her to see if she was ready to make their appearance and she was. So they exited her car and proceeded to the party. At that same time, Tico was dressed and left the house going to the party, it was a festive time.

The Drake was at the DJ booth asking everyone if his party was the bomb. As he said that he saw Blackman, they nodded at each other and Blackman's runners split up in the crowd to give free samples and sell the laced heroine and crack joints to everyone at discounted prices.

As Duck and Sharon made their way through the crowd, Duck could tell by all the admiring glances he had a 'dime piece' (which was Sharon). After hitting one of the booths to get her something to eat, Duck got a cup of beer to sip on.

Duck and Sharon ran into Cheryl and Clifton. They greeted each other and both couples continued on their way, Cheryl wondering silently where Duck got that pretty girl from. Cheryl's attention was drawn to all the women so was Clinton.  She said nothing, just taking it all in.

Tico was searching for Cheryl, he would walk the party all night if he had to.

Sergant caught up to Sagrin and the kids and they walked hand in hand through the party with the kids in tow.

One of the runners found a guy with his hand out for a tester joint and to seem like he wasn't broke, he took the tester and gave the runner five dollars for another. Him and his old lady immediately fired their shit up and it was pure utopia and they bragged about it to anyone that would listen.

Tico finally found Cheryl and Clifton but she was standing to the side as Clifton tried to win her a stuffed animal. Tico came up behind her and whispered, 'She was the finest woman at the party'. She turned around and Tico looked better than she remembered. Before her and Tico could say much, Clifton interrupted her thoughts with this big stuffed animal and glared at Tico, man did he hate this guy.

Tico made up a story of looking for the girl he was with but Clifton didn't believe him and kinda pulled Cheryl away heading deeper into the party. As Cheryl walked away she looked at Tico in his best outfit and thought about how great he looked.

Clifton broke her train of thought by asking her to dance. He knew she was thinking about Tico and he wanted to stop that thought. Right then the Drake wanted everyone to hustle and, if you never saw an entire block hustle, it was a sight to see. The Drake even joined the dance.

At this time, Duck was ready to fuck Sharon and she was all for it. Tico saw Duck and tried to kick it with him but he pointed his head at Sharon and Tico understood exactly what Duck was saying, without them exchanging a word. Duck was walking fast to leave the Block Party, he had bigger and better things waiting for him – Sharon!

Duck and Sharon got back into her car and drove to her house with her giving Duck the directions. She had a bomb plush spot. Duck just kept thanking God for his good fortune. When Duck and Sharon entered her spot, she started dropping clothes at the front door, Duck grabbed her and kissed her passionately. Sharon backed off teasingly and headed for the shower and Duck followed her feeling blessed, good sex, hell any sex at this time is good sex. Duck had waited long enough and he fucked Sharon in the shower, she loved it even though Duck wasn't her kind of man, he was a man and that would do.

The Block Party raged on till the wee hours of the morning. Everyone was straight and happy, high, drunk or both and fucking each other. Tico found a jump off to hit (a girl to fuck). The girl was cute but it just wasn't Cheryl so after he was done he told the girl he had to go to work. He lied, Tico just didn't want to stay there overnight.

Duck was fucking for all he was worth, he was going to make Sharon his that morning and when he was done he had a blissful sleep in her feather bed.

When he woke he had to pee but his dick was sore. As he tried to pee his dick was on fire and he screamed in sheer agony. Sharon had been cooking breakfast. She heard Duck holler and she rushed to see what the problem was. She opened the bathroom door and she saw Duck bent over with his hands on this thighs and his face twisted in pain. Sharon put her arms around Duck's shoulders and sat him on the side of the tub and she asked what happened.

Duck thought of a fast lie and said he stubbed his toe on the iron bath tub, he could never tell her he might have given her some kind of venereal disease. She would drop his ass like he was on fire! Duck thought about making up a story to leave and go to the Doctor but he convinced himself he could buy some pills from someone and all this would go away.

# Part 2 of The Blocks

The party was a success. The Drake and Blackman were heros just about in the dope gang now because they had the best main run. There was nothing or no one that could top them in Detroit at that time.

The party was a booming success with at least 1,000-1,500 new customers. Everyone trying to catch that same high that they got the first time that they tried.

The Drake messed up.